Railway Series, No. 3

JAMES THE RED ENGINE

by

THE REV. W. AWDRY

With illustrations by
C. REGINALD DALBY

KAYE & WARD LTD

First published by
Edmund Ward (Publishers) Ltd 1948
First paperback edition 1969 by Kaye & Ward Ltd
The Windmill Press, Kingswood, Tadworth, Surrey
Third impression 1985

Copyright 1948 Edmund Ward (Publishers) Ltd
Copyright © 1970 Kaye & Ward Ltd

ISBN 0 7182 1055 7

Printed and bound in Great Britain by
William Clowes Limited, Beccles and London

Dear Friends of Edward, Gordon, Henry
    and Thomas,

Thank you for your kind letters; here is the new book for which you asked.

James, who crashed into the story of *Thomas, the Tank Engine*, settles down and becomes a useful engine.

We are nationalised now, but the same engines still work the Region. I am glad, too, to tell you that the Fat Director, who understands our friends' ways, is still in charge, but is now the Fat Controller.

I hope you will enjoy this book too.

The Author

James and the Top-Hat

JAMES was a new engine who lived at a station at the other end of the line. He had two small wheels in front and six driving wheels behind. They weren't as big as Gordon's, and they weren't as small as Thomas's.

"You're a special Mixed-Traffic engine," the Fat Controller told him. "You'll be able to pull coaches or trucks quite easily."

But trucks are not easy things to manage and on his first day they had pushed him down a hill into a field.

He had been ill after the accident, but now he had new brakes and a shining coat of red paint.

"The red paint will cheer you up after your accident," said the Fat Controller kindly. "You are to pull coaches today, and Edward shall help you."

They went together to find the coaches.

"Be careful with the coaches, James," said Edward, "they don't like being bumped. Trucks are silly and noisy; they need to be bumped and taught to behave, but coaches get cross and will pay you out."

They took the coaches to the platform and were both coupled on in front. The Fat Controller, the Station-Master, and some little boys all came to admire James's shining rods and red paint.

James was pleased. "I am a really splendid engine," he thought, and suddenly let off steam. "Whee—ee—ee—ee—eesh!"

The Fat Controller, the Station-Master and the guard all jumped, and a shower of water fell on the Fat Controller's nice new top-hat.

Just then the whistle blew and James thought they had better go—so they went!

"Go on, go on," he puffed to Edward.

"Don't push, don't push," puffed Edward, for he did not like starting quickly.

"Don't go so fast, don't go so fast," grumbled the coaches; but James did not listen. He wanted to run away before the Fat Controller could call him back.

He didn't even want to stop at the first station. Edward tried hard to stop, but the two coaches in front were beyond the platform before they stopped, and they had to go back to let the passengers get out.

Lots of people came to look at James, and, as no one seemed to know about the Fat Controller's top-hat, James felt happier.

Presently they came to the junction where Thomas was waiting with his two coaches.

"Hullo, James!" said Thomas kindly, "feeling better? That's right. Ah! that's my guard's whistle. I must go. Sorry I can't stop. I don't know what the Fat Controller would do without me to run this branch line," and he puffed off importantly with his two coaches into a tunnel.

Leaving the junction, they passed the field where James had had his accident. The fence was mended and the cows were back again. James whistled, but they paid no attention.

They clattered through Edward's station-yard and started to climb the hill beyond.

"It's ever so steep, it's ever so steep," puffed James.

"I've done it before, I've done it before," puffed Edward.

"It's steep, but we'll do it—it's steep, but we'll do it," the two engines puffed together as they pulled the train up the long hill.

They both rested at the next station; Edward told James how Gordon had stuck on the hill, and he had had to push him up!

James laughed so much that he got hiccoughs and surprised an old lady in a black bonnet.

She dropped all her parcels, and three porters, the Station-Master and the guard had to run after her picking them up!

James was quiet in the shed that night. He had enjoyed his day, but he was a little afraid of what the Fat Controller would say about the top-hat!

James and the Boot-lace

NEXT morning the Fat Controller spoke severely to James: "If you can't behave, I shall take away your red coat and have you painted blue."

James did not like that at all and he was very rough with the coaches as he brought them to the platform.

"Come along, come along," he called rudely.

"All in good time, all in good time," the coaches grumbled.

"Don't talk, come on!" answered James, and with the coaches squealing and grumbling after him, he snorted into the station.

James *was* cross that morning. The Fat Controller had spoken to him, the coaches had dawdled and, worst of all, he had had to fetch his own coaches.

"Gordon never does," thought James, "and he is only painted blue. A splendid Red Engine like me should never have to fetch his own coaches." And he puffed and snorted round to the front of the train, and backed on to it with a rude bump.

"O—ooooh!" groaned the coaches, "that was too bad!"

To make James even more cross, he then had to take the coaches to a different platform, where no one came near him as he stood there. The Fat Controller was in his office, the Station-Master was at the other end of the train with the guard, and even the little boys stood a long way off.

James felt lonely. "I'll show them!" he said to himself. "They think Gordon is the only engine who can pull coaches."

And as soon as the guard's whistle blew, he started off with a tremendous jerk.

"Come on!—come on!—come on!" he puffed, and the coaches, squeaking and groaning in protest, clattered over the points on to the open line.

"Hurry!—hurry!—hurry!" puffed James.

"You're going too fast, you're going too fast," said the coaches, and indeed they were going so fast that they swayed from side to side.

James laughed and tried to go faster, but the coaches wouldn't let him.

"We're going to stop—we're going to stop—we're——going——to——stop," they said and James found himself going slower and slower.

"What's the matter?" James asked his driver.

"The brakes are hard on—leak in the pipe most likely. You've banged the coaches enough to make a leak in anything."

The guard and the driver got down and looked at the brake pipes all along the train.

At last they found a hole where rough treatment had made a joint work loose.

"How shall we mend it?" said the guard.

James's driver thought for a moment.

"We'll do it with newspapers and a leather boot-lace."

"Well, where is the boot-lace coming from?" asked the guard. "We haven't one."

"Ask the passengers," said the driver.

So the guard made everyone get out.

"Has anybody got a leather boot-lace?" he asked.

They all said "No" except one man in a bowler hat (whose name was Jeremiah Jobling) who tried to hide his feet.

"You have a leather boot-lace there I see, sir," said the guard. "Please give it to me."

"I won't," said Jeremiah Jobling.

"Then," said the guard sternly, "I'm afraid this train will just stop where it is."

Then the passengers all told the guard, the driver and the fireman what a Bad Railway it was. But the guard climbed into his van, and the driver and fireman made James let off steam. So they all told Jeremiah Jobling he was a Bad Man instead.

At last he gave them his laces, the driver tied a pad of newspapers tightly round the hole, and James was able to pull the train.

But he was a sadder and a wiser James and took care never to bump coaches again.

Troublesome Trucks

JAMES did not see the Fat Controller for several days. They left James alone in the shed, and did not even allow him to go out and push coaches and trucks in the yard.

"Oh, dear!" he thought sadly, "I'll never be allowed out any more; I shall have to stay in this shed for always, and no one will ever see my red coat again. Oh, dear! Oh, dear!" James began to cry.

Just then the Fat Controller came along.

"I see you are sorry, James," he said. "I hope, now, that you will be a better Engine. You have given me a lot of trouble. People are laughing at my Railway, and I do not like that at all."

"I am very sorry, sir," said James. "I will try hard to behave."

"That's a good engine," said the Fat Controller kindly. "I want you to pull some trucks for me. Run along and find them."

So James puffed happily away.

"Here are your trucks, James," said a little tank engine. "Have you got some boot-laces ready?" And he ran off laughing rudely.

"Oh! Oh! Oh!" said the trucks, as James backed down on them. "We want a proper engine, not a Red Monster."

James took no notice and started as soon as the guard was ready.

"Come along, come along," he puffed.

"We won't! We won't!" screamed the trucks.

But James didn't care, and he pulled the screeching trucks sternly out of the yard.

The trucks tried hard to make him give up, but he still kept on.

Sometimes their brakes would slip "on", and sometimes their axles would "run hot". Each time they would have to stop and put the trouble right, and each time James would start again, determined not to let the trucks beat him.

"Give up! give up! you can't pull us! You can't! You can't!" called the trucks.

"I can and I will! I can and I will!" puffed James.

And slowly but surely he pulled them along the line.

At last they saw Gordon's hill ahead.

"Look out for trouble, James," warned his driver. "We'll go fast and get them up before they know it. Don't let them stop you."

So James went faster, and they were soon halfway up the hill.

"I'm doing it! I'm doing it!" he panted.

But it was hard work.

"Will the top never come?" he thought, when with a sudden jerk it all came easier.

"I've done it! I've done it!" he puffed triumphantly.

"Hurrah!" he thought, "it's easy now." But his driver shut off steam.

"They've done it again," he said. "We've left our tail behind!"

The last ten trucks were running backwards down the hill. The coupling had snapped!

But the guard was brave. Very carefully and cleverly he made them stop. Then he got out and walked down the line with his red flag.

"That's why it was easy," said James as he backed the other trucks carefully down. "What silly things trucks are! There might have been an accident."

Meanwhile the guard had stopped Edward who was pulling three coaches.

"Shall I help you, James?" called Edward.

"No, thank you," answered James, "I'll pull them myself."

"Good, don't let them beat you."

So James got ready. Then with a "peep, peep" he was off.

"I *can* do it, I *can* do it," he puffed. He pulled and puffed as hard as he could.

"Peep pip peep peep! You're doing well!" whistled Edward, as James slowly struggled up the hill, with clouds of smoke and steam pouring from his funnel.

"I've done it, I've done it," he panted and disappeared over the top.

They reached their station safely. James was resting in the yard, when Edward puffed by with a cheerful "peep peep".

Then, walking towards him across the rails, James saw . . . the Fat Controller!

"Oh dear! What will he say?" he asked himself sadly.

But the Fat Controller was smiling. "I was in Edward's train, and saw everything," he said. "You've made the most troublesome trucks on the line behave. After that, you deserve to keep your red coat."

James and the Express

SOMETIMES Gordon and Henry slept in James's shed, and they would talk of nothing but boot-laces! James would talk about engines who got shut up in tunnels and stuck on hills, but they wouldn't listen, and went on talking and laughing.

"You talk too much, little James," Gordon would say. "A fine strong engine like me has something to talk about. I'm the only engine who can pull the Express. When I'm not there, they need two engines. Think of that!

"I've pulled expresses for years, and have never once lost my way. I seem to know the right line by instinct," said Gordon proudly. Every wise engine knows, of course, that the signalman works the points to make engines run on the right lines, but Gordon was so proud that he had forgotten.

"Wake up, James," he said next morning, "it's nearly time for the Express. What are you doing?—Odd jobs? Ah well! We all have to begin somewhere, don't we? Run along now and get my coaches—don't be late now."

James went to get Gordon's coaches. They were now all shining with lovely new paint. He was careful not to bump them, and they followed him smoothly into the station singing happily. "We're going away, we're going away."

"I wish I was going with you," said James. "I should love to pull the Express and go flying along the line."

He left them in the station and went back to the yard, just as Gordon with much noise and blowing of steam backed on to the train.

The Fat Controller was on the train with other Important People, and, as soon as they heard the guard's whistle, Gordon started.

"Look at me now! Look at me now!" he puffed, and the coaches glided after him out of the station.

"Poop poop poo poo poop!—Good-bye little James! See you tomorrow."

James watched the train disappear round a curve, and then went back to work. He pushed some trucks into their proper sidings and went to fetch the coaches for another train.

He brought the coaches to the platform and was just being uncoupled when he heard a mournful, quiet "Shush shush shush shush!" and there was Gordon trying to sidle into the station without being noticed.

"Hullo, Gordon! Is it tomorrow?" asked James. Gordon didn't answer; he just let off steam feebly.

"Did you lose your way, Gordon?"

"No, it was lost for me," he answered crossly, "I was switched off the main line on to the loop; I had to go all round and back again."

"Perhaps it was instinct," said James brightly.

Meanwhile all the passengers hurried to the booking office. "We want our money back," they shouted.

Everyone was making a noise, but the Fat Controller climbed on a trolley and blew the guard's whistle so loudly that they all stopped to look at him.

Then he promised them a new train at once.

"Gordon can't do it," he said. "Will you pull it for us, James?"

"Yes, sir, I'll try."

So James was coupled on and everyone got in again.

"Do your best, James," said the Fat Controller kindly. Just then the whistle blew and he had to run to get in.

"Come along, come along," puffed James.

"You're pulling us well! you're pulling us well," sang the coaches.

"Hurry, hurry, hurry," puffed James.

Stations and bridges flashed by, the passengers leaned out of the windows and cheered, and they soon reached the terminus.

Everyone said "Thank you" to James. "Well done," said the Fat Controller. "Would you like to pull the Express sometimes?"

"Yes, please," answered James happily.

Next day when James came by, Gordon was pushing trucks in the yard.

"I like some quiet work for a change," he said. "I'm teaching these trucks manners. You did well with those coaches I hear . . . good, we'll show them!" and he gave his trucks a bump, making them cry, "Oh! Oh! Oh! Oh!"

James and Gordon are now good friends. James sometimes takes the Express to give Gordon a rest. Gordon never talks about bootlaces, and they are both quite agreed on the subject of trucks!

The Rev. W. Awdry Railway Series

POP-UP BOOKS

Eight titles now available with paper mechanics by Roy Laming and pictures by Clive Spong.

Thomas the Tank Engine Goes Fishing
Bertie the Bus and Thomas the Tank Engine
Henry the Green Engine Gets Out
The Flying Kipper and Henry the Green Engine
James the Red Engine and the Troublesome Trucks
Thomas the Tank Engine and the Tractor
Percy the Small Engine Takes the Plunge
Henry the Green Engine and the Elephant

MAP OF THE ISLAND OF SODOR

Sodor, situated between Barrow-in-Furness and the Isle of Man is where Thomas, Henry, James, Edward, Gordon and the other engines have their adventures. This colourful map, measuring 560 × 760 mm when open, makes an excellent wall decoration. There is a key to many of the places where incidents in the books take place.